This
PJ BOOK
belongs to

_____

_____

JEWISH BEDTIME STORIES and SONGS

TEA WITH ZAYDE

BARNEY SALTZBERG

A NEAL PORTER BOOK
ROARING BROOK PRESS
NEW YORK

For Ella and her Baba Irv,
who gave his family the gifts of story, laughter, and love

Library of Congress Cataloging-in-Publication Data
Saltzberg, Barney, author, illustrator.
Tea with Grandpa / Barney Saltzberg. — First edition.
pages cm
"A Neal Porter Book."
Summary: No matter how far apart they are, a little girl and her
grandfather share a cup of tea every day at half past three.
ISBN 978-1-59643-894-1 (hardcover)
[1. Stories in rhyme. 2. Grandfathers—Fiction. 3. Tea—Fiction. 4.
Internet—Fiction.] I. Title.
PZ8.3.S174Te 2014
[E]—dc23

2013001548

Roaring Brook Press books may be purchased for business or promotional use.
For information on bulk purchases please contact Macmillan Corporate and Premium Sales Department
at (800) 221-7945 x5442 or by email at specialmarkets@macmillan.com.

First edition 2014
Book design by Jennifer Browne
Printed in China by 1010 Printing International Limited, North Point, Hong Kong

3   5   7   9   10   8   6   4   2
ISBN 978-1-62672-599-7 (PJ Library edition)
Code 201625K/B0823/Grandparent

Every day
at half past three . . .

Me and Zayde.
Time for tea.

I can pour
so carefully.

Zayde holds his cup for me.

He tells
me stories.

I sing a song.

Zayde laughs
and sings along.

When I dance . . .

He laughs
some more.

I am a lion,

RO . . . RO . . . ROAR!

"I'd like some muffin," he will say.

I have to tell him,
"Too far away."

We clink our cups . . .

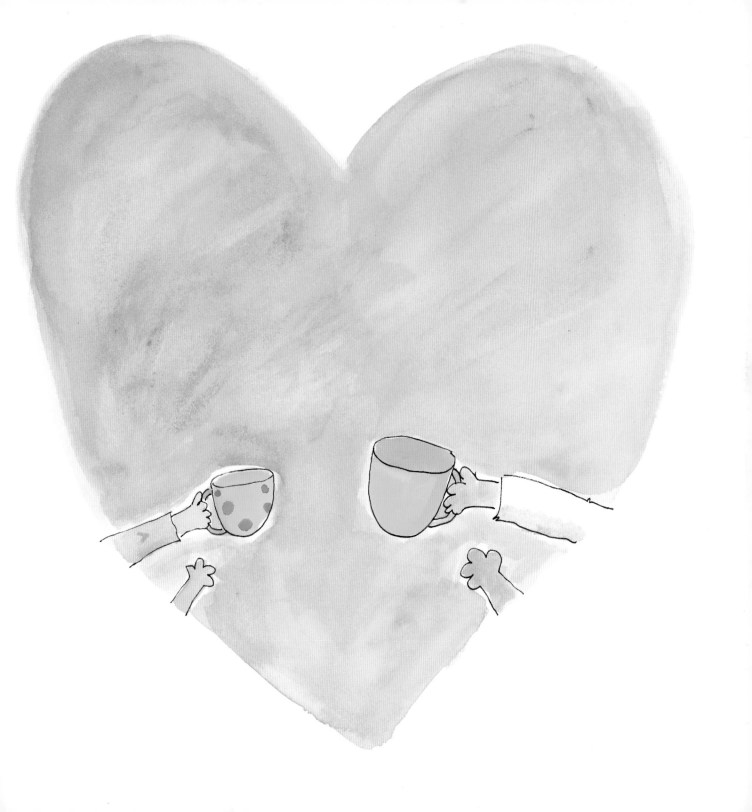

I say "Good-bye."

He says,
"Tomorrow,
sweetie pie."

'Cause every day
at half past
three . . .

Me and Zayde,
time for tea.